Amanda and the Witch Switch

Amanda and the Witch Switch

Story and Pictures by
John Himmelman

VIKING KESTREL

VIKING KESTREL
Viking Penguin Inc., 40 West 23rd Street, New York, New York 10010, U.S.A.
Penguin Books Ltd, Harmondsworth, Middlesex, England
Penguin Books Australia Ltd, Ringwood, Victoria, Australia
Penguin Books Canada Limited, 2801 John Street, Markham, Ontario, Canada L3R 1B4
Penguin Books (N.Z.) Ltd, 182–190 Wairau Road, Auckland 10, New Zealand

Copyright © John Himmelman, 1985   All rights reserved
First published in 1985 by Viking Penguin Inc.
Published simultaneously in Canada

Library of Congress Cataloging in Publication Data
Himmelman, John.   Amanda and the witch switch.
Summary: A friendly witch named Amanda gives a toad three wishes, but her
good intentions backfire when he uses one of the wishes to become a witch,
1. Children's stories, American.   [1. Witches—Fiction.   2. Toads—Fiction]   I. Title.
PZ7.H5686Am   1985   [E]   84-19515   ISBN 0-670-11531-2

Printed in Japan by Dai Nippon   1   2   3   4   5   89   88   87   86   85
Set in Bookman Light.

This book is dedicated to Mom,
and to my fond memories
of Grandma Nault.

Up in the hills,

deep in the forest,

there lived a friendly old witch.
Her name was Amanda.

One morning while she was rocking
in her chair, she decided it was too
lovely a day to spend indoors.

Amanda stepped outside and stretched.
"What a beautiful day it is," she said.
"Today I will do something extra nice!"

She added some flowers here and there,

taught some beavers how to boogie,

and some trees how to sing,

but that still didn't seem like enough.

Then she came upon a little toad
sitting on a rock.

"My name is Amanda," she said,
"and it is such a nice day today
that I will make three of your wishes
come true."

"Okay," said the toad.

"Make me a prince."

"Sorry, I can only do that for frogs,"
she answered.

"All right then," said the toad.
"Make me a witch, like yourself."
Amanda thought for a moment.
"Well, I suppose I could," and *POOF!*

The toad turned into a witch!

Then the toad pointed to Amanda.
"And now I want *you* to turn into a toad."

and *POOF!*

Amanda was turned into a toad.

Amanda sat there *looking* helpless
as the toad went off into the forest.
"Now I can do any magic I want," he said.

He turned a pond into mud,

made a deer's antlers into flowers,

turned some rocks into marshmallows,

and made some rabbits turn purple.

He made a bear the size of a bee

and a bee the size of a bear.

But this last prank backfired,
and the bee went after the toad!

I'll just turn myself back into a toad
and threaten to eat him if he doesn't
put me down, he thought.

But this didn't quite work out the way
he planned.
"*Help,*" he called to Amanda.
"*Please help me!*"

I guess he's learned his lesson,
thought Amanda, and she turned the bee
back to normal size.

"Well, you still have one more wish,"
she said to the toad.

"I wish everything was back
the way it was," he said.

"I thought you would," said Amanda,
and she turned everything back to normal.

Well, almost everything.